To
PAUL HELLER,
my
favorite
English teacher

Copyright © 1988 by Ruth Heller. All rights reserved.
Published by Grosset & Dunlap, Inc., a member of The Putnam
& Grosset Group, New York. Published simultaneously in Canada.
GROSSET & DUNLAP is a trademark of Grosset & Dunlap, Inc.
Sandcastle Books and the Sandcastle logo are trademarks belonging to
The Putnam & Grosset Group. First Sandcastle Books edition, 1992.
Printed in Hong Kong. Library of Congress Catalog Card Number: 87-82718
ISBN (hardcover) 0-448-10480-6 G H I J
ISBN (Sandcastle) 0-448-40452-4 E F G H I J

Kites Sail High
A Book About Verbs

Written and illustrated by
RUTH HELLER

GROSSET & DUNLAP, NEW YORK

A VERB is really the most superb
of any word you've ever heard....

Verbs tell you
something's
being done.

Roses
BLOOM

and
people
RUN.

Pelicans
FLY,

kites
SAIL
high

and rabbits
quickly
MULTIPLY.

A
VIGOROUS
VERB
is
super superb.

It
tells you
fireworks
EXPLODE

or
horses
THUNDER
down
the
road.

Of
equal
attraction
are
verbs
of
less
action.

Have
is
a
verb.

These kings **HAVE** gold.

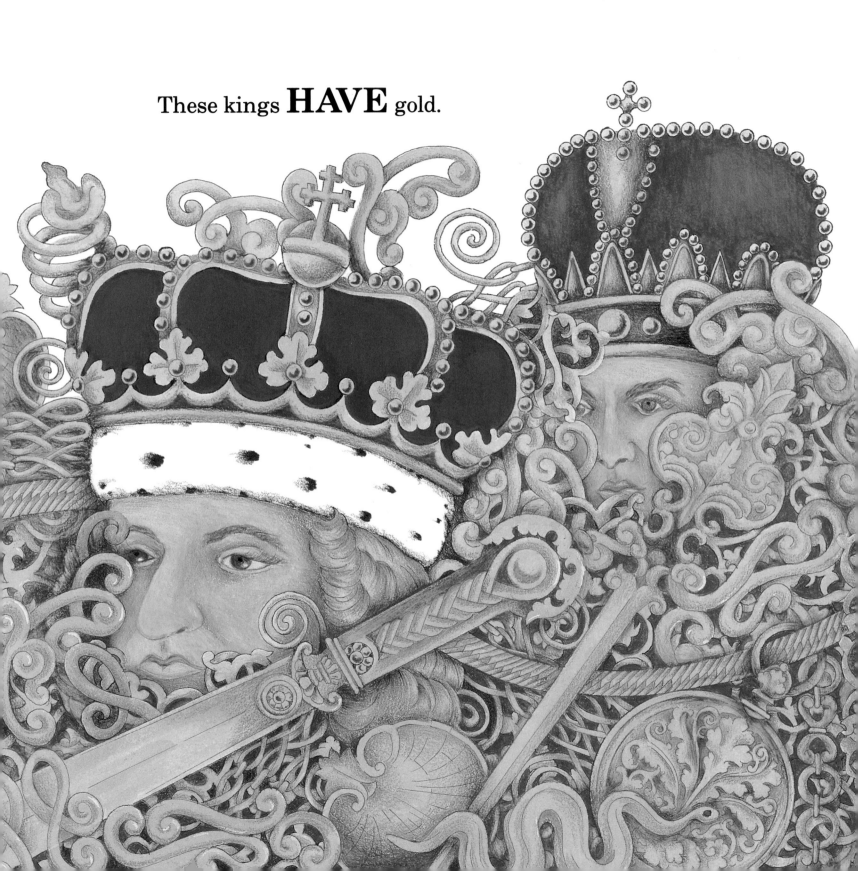

And so is has.

She **HAS** a cold.

Here are verbs we use to link.

I **AM** a cat. My nose **IS** pink.

My fur **FEELS** soft.
I **SOUND** content.
My lifestyle
LOOKS
most opulent.

IS, AM and **ARE,** and **WAS** and **WERE,**
and **BEING, BEEN** and **BE**
are LINKING VERBS and, as you see,
show no activity.

Nor do these other verbs that link—
FEEL
or **SOUND**
or **LOOK.**

(More of them
are listed
as you open up
this book.)

IS, AM and ARE
and
WAS and WERE
and
BEING, BEEN and BE
are here again.

This time, you'll see,
they're called
AUX • IL • I • AR • Y

along with
DO
and
DOES and DID
and
HAS and HAVE
and
HAD
and
SHALL and WILL
and also
SHOULD
and
MIGHT and MAY
and
CAN and WOULD.

They're HELPING VERBS, and they are able
to form VERB PHRASES, as in this fable:

While the hare,
who
SHOULD HAVE WON,
WAS NAPPING
in the noonday sun,
the tortoise,
with a steady pace,
WAS INCHING
by
and won
the race.

Only a verb can change its TENSES, and
here are some of the consequences....

IRREGULAR
VERBS
leave you aghast
by the way
they
change
from
present
to
past—

*I
write
I
wrote
or
I
have
written*

I BITE, I BIT or I HAVE BITTEN
I SINK, I SANK or I HAVE SUNK
I SHRINK, I SHRANK or I HAVE SHRUNK

(These are just a very few from a list of more than fifty-two.)

Most
REGULAR
VERBS
change
easily
by
adding on
an
"e"
and
"d"…

I
PAINT

I
PAINTED
or

I
**HAVE
PAINTED.**

There
are
three
MOODS
to be
expressed,
and
of course
it's
the verb
that does
this
the best.

The
IMPERATIVE
MOOD
makes
a
request.

Please **TAKE** just one…

and **LEAVE** the rest.

Or it gives a command.

MARCH!

This
is
a
whole
sentence
in
one
single
word,
and
of course
this can only
be done by
a
verb.

The
INDICATIVE
MOOD
just
states
a
fact—

We
ACT.

The SUBJUNCTIVE MOOD expresses a wish...

or
uses
the words
"as though"
or
"if."

If
I
WERE
a
fish,

as though that
COULD BE,

I'd
SWIM
in a
beautiful
tropical
sea.

Verbs have two VOICES,
PASSIVE and...

This
egg
**WAS
LAID**
by
a
hen
named
Sade.

ACTIVE.

Choose the one
you find more attractive—

A
hen
named
Sade
LAID
this
egg.

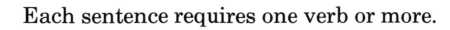

Each sentence requires one verb or more.

She
SELLS
sea shells
at
the
seashore.

And
here
is
a
sentence
with
verbs
galore....

Lizards **LEAP**
and **PILE**
in a heap
and **SLITHER**...

and
CLIMB
and
SPLASH
and
CREEP
and
SWIM
and
CAVORT
and
FALL
asleep.

Now
as an important
afterthought
about
words that are
VERBS
and words that are not ...

"Is"
is a verb.
"Not"
is not.

Put them together,
you have
"is not."

Then
with a quick
converging action,
"is not" becomes "isn't."
That's called
a CONTRACTION.

Is not becomes isn't.

Use every restraint
and
never, no never,
please,
never say

ain't